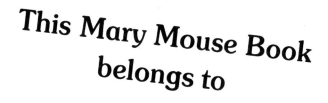

This Mary Mouse Book
belongs to

....

....

date ....

Enid Blyton

MARY MOUSE AND THE DOLL FAMILY

RAVETTE BOOKS

Do you remember little Mary Mouse?
She went to live with the Doll family in
the Dolls' House. There she helped Mummy
Doll and Daddy Doll look after their three
children, Melia, Tom and Jamie.

Each morning Mary Mouse was up early.
While Mummy and Daddy Doll made
breakfast Mary dressed the children and
brushed their hair.

Then she went shopping and took the children with her. Baby Jamie went to sleep and did not wake even when Mary Mouse piled the shopping into the pushchair.

After lunch Mummy and Daddy Doll went
out and Mary played with the children.

When Mummy and Daddy Doll came home they all had tea together. Then Mary told the three children stories until it was time for bed and she kissed them goodnight.

Soon Mary Mouse was quite one of the family. She found Daddy Doll's glasses when he lost them, which was about three times a day.

She comforted Melia when she fell down and hurt her knee. She scolded Tom when he tore his shorts and made a big hole.

And she taught Jamie to walk. He followed
Mary everywhere, holding on to her apron
strings.

Melia had a birthday coming soon. She asked Mary if she could have a party. "Of course," said Mary. "You shall have the best party anyone ever had!"

So when they were out for a walk and met Teddy the Bear, they asked him to come. And Peter the Penguin. And Pom the Panda. And Benny the Blue Cat.

Then Mary made all the cakes and jellies.
There were dozens and dozens, all shapes
and sizes and there was a marvellous
birthday cake with icing and five candles for
Melia. There were boxes of crackers too and
Mary hoped Jamie wouldn't mind the bangs.

She helped Melia put on a new dress and tied her hair with a big red bow. Tom wore a new suit with blue and green stripes and Mary dressed Jamie up in a new yellow jumpsuit. He did look sweet.

Mummy and Daddy Doll were dressed up too
and Mary Mouse put on a special party bow
and a beautiful blue lace dress.
"You look sweet, Mary," cried the children
and they hugged her.

Then the guests came. First Teddy the Bear and then Peter the Penguin. Then Pom the Panda with Benny the Blue Cat. They all brought Melia presents.

Then they sat down to tea. Teddy the Bear ate sixteen cakes, fourteen sandwiches and two jellies. He got very fat and burst a button off his best waistcoat. After that he didn't eat any more.

Melia cut her birthday cake when the candles were lighted. It looked lovely. Everyone had a piece and Melia made Mary have the biggest!

Then they had the crackers. Jamie didn't mind the bangs at all and Mary *was* proud of him when he pulled one with her! Everyone looked very funny in their paper hats.

Then they played games. First they played
musical chairs, then hunt-the-thimble.
Mary put the thimble on Jamie's head,
and nobody saw it for a long time. Then
Pom the Panda found it.

At last it was time to go home. The guests said goodbye and thank you very much.

Mary put the three tired children to bed.
"Thank you for a lovely day," they said.

"It was a great success," said Mummy Doll.
"What would we do without you."

"I'm the happiest mouse in the world!"
said Mary Mouse as she got into bed.
And she really was!

Other Mary Mouse titles in this series:

MARY MOUSE AND THE DOLLS' HOUSE
MARY MOUSE ON HOLIDAY
HALLO MARY MOUSE

Series Editor Sue Hook
Designed and illustrated by **Gloria**

First published by Ravette Books Limited 1988

Printed and bound in Great Britain
for Ravette Books Limited, 3 Glenside Estate,
Star Road, Partridge Green,
Horsham, Sussex RH13 8RA
by Purnell Book Production Limited,
Paulton, Bristol BS18 5LQ

ISBN 1 85304 019 3